WHAT WILL HAPPEN NEXT?

You trudge wearily upon the beach wondering whether you will ever find food decent enough to eat. You walk on into the meadow. You know you could never make it up the rocky hill. The hot sun beats down on your head. You feel faint and fall unconscious on the ground. Sometime later you wake up and notice a long, mean-looking snake, covered with diamond-shaped patches. It is slithering across your legs. . . .

The next adventure is up to you. If you decide to try to jump away, you turn to page 13, and if you decide to lie very still and hope the snake slithers away, you turn to page 15. But remember! Think before you act—one mistake can be your last on Sugarcane Island!

Sugarcane Island

by Edward Packard

Illustrated by Barbara Carter

AN ARCHWAY PAPERBACK
POCKET BOOKS . NEW YORK

POCKET BOOKS, a Simon & Schuster division of
GULF & WESTERN CORPORATION
1230 Avenue of the Americas, New York, N.Y. 10020

Published by arrangement with Vermont Crossroads Press
Library of Congress Catalog Card Number: 76-6039

ISBN: 0-671-56104-9

First Pocket Books printing March, 1978

10 9 8 7 6 5 4 3

AN ARCHWAY PAPERBACK and ARCH are trademarks
of Simon & Schuster.

Printed in the U.S.A.

IL 3+

Sugarcane Island

IMPORTANT

Do not read this book straight through from beginning to end. These pages contain many different adventures a person might have on Sugarcane Island. But the adventures you have will be affected by the decisions you make.

From time to time as you read along, you will have to make a choice. Then follow the instructions to see what happens to you next.

REMEMBER!

Think before you act.
One mistake can be your last—on
Sugarcane Island.

You stand on the deck of a large boat looking back at the Golden Gate Bridge, as you set out into the Pacific Ocean. You have been invited to join Doctor Carleton Frisbee on an expedition to the Galapagos Islands. Dr. Frisbee studies turtles for zoos. He knows everything about turtles.

The trip is great fun. But one day, as the boat is sailing along through the churning waters and you are stretched out in your deck chair watching the flying fish, you see a huge wave heading toward the boat.

The wave was caused by an earthquake somewhere on the ocean floor. It rolls across the water at you. Your boat rises with it, higher and higher. Then the foaming water sweeps across the deck. It is too late to run, and all you can do is grab hold of your deck chair.

In a moment you are carried right off your boat, clinging high on the crest, riding the great wave, flying on a cloud of water. The only thing you can see through the foam and spray are your own hands tightly gripping the deck chair. Then you feel yourself sliding down the back of the wave. The next thing you remember is waking from a deep sleep.

You wonder if you have been dreaming. You know you have not. Instead of being back in your bed, you find yourself lying high on a huge sand dune. Behind you is a broad, sloping beach. You watch the foaming waves thrashing upon it. Ahead of you is a meadow of tall reeds bounded by high rocky hills. You are hungry and thirsty. You look out at the ocean and see nothing but endless blue water. Except for a few sea gulls hovering over the waves, you are all alone.

If you decide to walk along the beach, turn to page 5.

If you decide to climb the rocky hill, turn to page 6.

You walk along the beach. The sand is so soft and hot on your bare feet that you go down to the edge of the sea, where the sand feels cool and firm. You walk on and on, but each new stretch of beach seems like the last. You are thirsty and hungry and so tired that you can hardly walk. Then, almost under foot, you see water spouting out of the sand. You dig down and pull up a clam and then another. You break the shells and pick out the meaty part. It doesn't look very tasty.

If you decide to eat the clams, turn to page 7.

If you decide not to eat the clams, turn to page 8.

You head up toward the rocky hill, crossing a marshy meadow on the way. You watch carefully for snakes. You find some tasty berries that quench your thirst and make you feel stronger. You walk on, climbing higher. But you find that to get to the top of the hill, you will have to climb up some steep and dangerous looking rocks.

If you decide to try to climb the steep rocks, turn to page 9.

If you decide to go back to the berries and rest for the night, turn to page 10.

The first bite tastes awful, but it makes you realize how hungry you are. You eat more clams, and they taste better. You feel stronger, but also thirstier. You run up the beach and into the forest, looking for water. You come upon a small pond. The water tastes salty.

If you decide to drink the water, turn to page 11.

If you decide not to drink the water, turn to page 12.

You trudge wearily upon the beach, wondering whether you will ever find food decent enough to eat. You walk on into the meadow. You know you could never make it up the rocky hill. The hot sun beats down on your head. You feel faint and fall unconscious on the ground. Sometime later you wake up and notice a long, mean-looking snake, covered with diamond-shaped patches. It is slithering across your legs.

If you decide to try to jump away, turn to page 13.

If you decide to lie very still and hope the snake slithers away, turn to page 15.

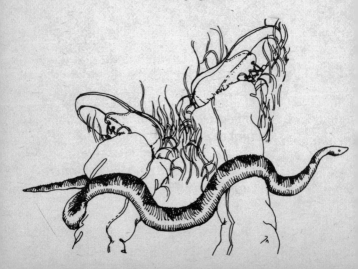

You start climbing the steep hill. It is rough going, and once you lose your grip and almost fall down a rock wall. Finally you reach the top. Ahead of you is a beautiful valley. Off to your left, you see smoke rising. To your right, you hear the sound of drum beats.

If you head toward the smoke, turn to page 16.

If you head toward the drums, turn to page 17.

You find your way back to the berries and munch on them hungrily. You know you need more than this to live on, yet you wonder whether you can find anything else to eat. You peer through some heavy brush looking for more berries. There, standing before you, is an enormous white dog.

If you go up to the dog, turn to page 18.

If you stay hidden, turn to page 19.

You drink some water: It tastes good but makes your stomach feel queasy. You know you must find something better than those clams and this water. You start walking along a path through the brush. Suddenly you see a large animal that looks like a tiger without any stripes. It has large pointed teeth. You wonder whether to try to climb a nearby tree or to stay still and hope that it will not see you or smell you.

If you decide to run for the tree, turn to page 20.

If you decide to stay very still, turn to page 21.

You walk on and on looking for good water. You become thirstier. You wonder whether you will ever find water. Then you look over a ledge and see a sparkling clear brook. A fierce looking pirate with a red beard and a brass ring in his ear is standing there fishing.

If you go down to the brook, turn to page 22.

If you stay hidden on the ledge, turn to page 23.

You pull your legs up in order to spring to your feet, but the snake lunges and sinks its fangs into your leg. The pain is terrible. You jump up and run away, but in a few seconds you faint and fall to the ground.

A long time later you wake up in a thatched hut. An island woman is standing over you. She gives you coconut milk. Your leg still hurts, but you feel better. The woman leaves. You look out and see fierce-looking islanders doing a wild tribal dance around a bonfire.

If you decide to run away, turn to
page 25.

If you decide to stay, turn to
page 26.

The snake slithers along over your legs and rustles into the brush. You quickly jump up and run off in the other direction, but suddenly you feel yourself slipping. You have fallen into a deep pit—an animal trap. You wait there wondering whether you will be rescued or whether an animal may fall in with you. After an hour or so some short, hairy, ape-like men arrive and peer down at you. They are very excited to find a person like you. Quickly they pull you out.

If you try to run off into the forest, and hide, turn to page 28.

If you try to make friends, turn to page 29.

You follow a long path toward the rising smoke. You chew at some sweet reeds growing along the trail. It is sugarcane! You feel happier. You continue on but suddenly stumble upon a pile of bones. They are scary looking.

If you continue further, turn to page 31.

If you turn back, turn to page 32.

You walk along the path through the woods. The drum beats pound in your ears louder and faster—thumpp, thummpp, thummmpp. Then you hear people singing and chanting. You reach the end of the woods. Ahead of you is a large clearing leading to a large village. You crawl through the brush so as to get a good view without being seen. There, only a hundred feet away, are hundreds of islanders in bright red and yellow costumes, dancing about wildly. It looks as if they are having a good time.

If you go into the village, turn to page 33.

If you continue on through the woods, turn to page 35.

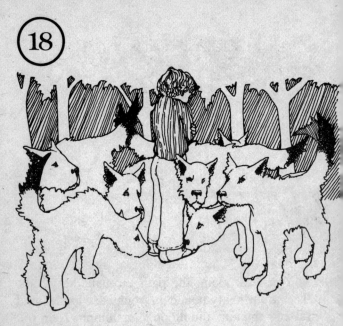

As soon as you go up to the dog, he runs around barking loudly. He does not bite, but nudges you along a path. When you try to step aside, he nips at your heels. You have no choice but to go along. After a while, another dog appears. They herd you onto a meadow where there are at least a dozen more of them. They come about and sniff you. It gives you a creepy feeling.

If you turn to run away, turn to page 36.

If you do not try to run away, turn to page 37.

The dog runs off after a rabbit. You run too—in the opposite direction—on and on through the tall, waving, brown grass. Just as you are about to drop from exhaustion, you come upon a fast flowing stream. The water is cool and clear. You drink eagerly. Across the stream you see hundreds of coconut trees.

If you attempt to swim the stream, turn to page 38.

If you do not attempt to swim the stream, turn to page 39.

You run for the tree. The beast sees you move and springs toward you. You leap at the lowest branch and swing up. The tree shudders as the beast crashes against it, but for the moment you are safe. It looks hungrily up at you. Then, as if startled by something unknown, it runs off. Soon after, a band of people with spears come along almost beneath your perch in the tree.

If you decide to call out and let them see you, turn to page 40.

If you decide to stay hidden in the tree, turn to page 41.

You hardly dare breathe as you sit there, waiting. Finally, after what seems like hours, the beast runs off into the forest. You walk out a few steps, but step into very soft ground. It is quicksand. In a moment you are stuck up to your knees. You can see that firm ground is only a few yards away.

If you try to walk out of the quicksand, turn to page 42.

If you throw yourself flat on your back and then roll toward firm ground, turn to page 43.

You walk up to the brook and take a long drink.

"Avast you lubber," says the pirate.

"Please, sir, do you have any food? I am very hungry," you say.

The pirate roars with laughter and points to some fish he has just caught.

"Eat some fish and I'll show you something better," he says. "But if you insult that fish by refusing to dine, I'll throw you to his brothers at nine."

If you eat the fish, turn to page 45.

If you refuse to eat the fish, turn to page 46.

The pirate soon collects the fish he has caught and leaves. You run down and take a long drink from the brook. Then you follow him to a hut in

the woods and, from a distance, watch him cook the fish. He sings a song:

"Tonight I have more fish to fry.
When will some tender flesh grace my eye?"

─────────────────────────────

If you decide to go up to the pirate, turn to page 47.

If you decide to hide in the woods, turn to page 49.

You dash out through the woods and come to a grove of tall coconut trees. You find some coconuts on the ground and crack them open on a sharp rock. They taste good. With new energy, you climb a high hill. From the top you see the broad sea sparkling with whitecaps. Suddenly a voice calls out:

"And who are you?"

You look around and through the trees see a lean-to. In it is an old bearded man with a wooden leg.

"Come here," he commands, waving a thick cane.

If you go up to the man, turn to page 50.

If you leave him and continue on, turn to page 51.

After a while, some islanders come into your hut. They bring with them a young warrior.

An old man comes up to you and says, "You must follow him. He take you over mountains to your tribe."

You have no choice, and you and the warrior set out on a long journey through the mountains. You walk along animal trails and sleep under the stars. One day you and the warrior climb up toward a ridge so high it is covered with snow. You are on a narrow path with a hundred foot drop on either side. Suddenly the warrior tries to push you off. You regain your balance, but you must get away.

If you run higher, turn to page 52.

If you run back down, turn to page 53.

You run off, but the hairy men quickly catch you. They take you back to their village and tie you to a stake. Everyone comes around and stares at you. Some people poke you with sticks. After a while, they feed you rice and tea. You are very tired. You lie down on the ground and soon fall asleep.

In the morning they give you a breakfast of coconuts and molasses cake. Then they take you to a swiftly flowing river and give you a small raft and a pole. You can hear the roaring rapids downstream. They urge you on to the raft.

If you set out on the river in the raft, turn to page 54.

If you sit down and refuse to go, turn to page 55.

The islanders take you back to their village. A family invites you into their hut for dinner. Afterward you sit with them as they play their flutes in front of a fire. They give you a soft mat on which to sleep and bid you good night. Next morning you are brought before the high chieftain. She speaks:

"Your coming is a lucky omen. It means no army will bother us. You will stay with us and be happy here in Abagun. Never try to leave."

You live with the family who was kind to you, and you find that life is good in Abagun. You learn how to hunt and to find plants to eat. You become tough and learn to run fast as a deer. Still, you feel homesick.

If you try to escape, turn to page 56.

If you stay, turn to page 57.

You continue on, but soon some mean people run out and grab you and take you away to a large hut. There, also held prisoner, is a sailor who was shipwrecked and captured.

"They will bury us unless we can show them a magic trick by noon tomorrow," he says.

You see that the guard has fallen asleep.

If you wait and try to think of a magic trick, turn to page 58.

If you try to escape, turn to page 60.

You turn back and head toward the sound of the drums. After a long time you come upon another pile of bones. You are only a hundred yards from the village of the drums.

Suddenly there is a crash of thunder and flashes of lightning. The wind roars and the rain pours.

If you run on into the village, turn to page 61.

If you hide under a rock ledge, turn to page 62.

As you walk into the village, the islanders surround you and start a new round of singing and dancing. Then they stop and everyone falls silent. The chief comes out. You shake hands with him and smile. He invites you to sit with him. Helpers bring a fried coconut, roast rabbit, sugarcane cake, cinnamon cookies, and lemonade.

One of the islanders at the table speaks to you. "Tomorrow," he says, "there will be a war with the other tribe. Can you help us?" Everyone looks to you. You can see that everyone fears that the other tribe will destroy the village.

If you say you'll help, turn to page 64.

If you say you can't help, turn to page 65.

You decide not to risk going into the village. You follow a path and find a sugarcane meadow. You munch on the sugarcane. It is good. Further along, you come upon a cave. Just inside the cave is an open chest. It is full or rubies, emeralds, and diamonds. You wonder why there is no one near-by.

If you decide to take some of the treasure and continue on, turn to page 66.

If you decide to hide and watch to see if anyone comes, turn to page 67.

You run through the woods. The dogs run after you, barking and growling. Your only chance is to dive into the river. You swim across it, leaving the howling dogs on the other side. You wander along through the woods and reach a clearing. Before you is a large hut with a thatched roof. In it are a group of strangely dressed women with pointed hats and great pots of boiling brews. One of them pulls you inside and says, "We've been waiting for you. Drink this secret potion."

If you drink the potion, turn to page 68.

If you refuse to drink the potion, turn to page 69.

The dogs mill about you, growling and nipping at each other's heels. Then they run howling off after some unseen game. You run in the other direction. Almost immediately you see up ahead a giant green turtle, hurrying along as if determined to get somewhere important.

If you climb on the turtle, turn to page 70.

If you just follow the turtle, turn to page 71.

38

You plunge into the cool water and swim for the opposite shore, but the current runs swiftly. You realize you could never swim all the way across. You clutch a log and hold on, as the current carries you downstream. The water bubbles and foams around you. Your log crashes into a rock. You are thrown off into the water, but you manage to scramble onto a mossy bank where you can look down on a waterfall. Near it you see some people making strange and pleasing music with instruments made from huge sea shells. They are eating pink fruit of a sort you have never seen before. You walk over to them and they give you some fruit. It tastes very, very good. You take more of the strange fruit and listen to their music.

Turn to page 72.

You lie by the river wondering what to do next. You look around. There seems to be nothing but thick jungle on one side, and a river full of crocodiles on the other. You work your way along the river bank and come to a steep, rocky hill. Then, somewhere behind you, an unknown animal roars. You must try to climb to safety.

Turn to page 9.

You call down "Hello there!" The people look up. They are astounded and begin to dance around under the tree. You jump down. They quickly seize you and lift you up and carry you back to their village. They lead you into a hut and give you some water. Several of them gather around you, scowling and mumbling. The tallest one stands on his head. The others glare at you.

If you decide to stand on your head, turn to page 73.

If you decide not to stand on your head, turn to page 74.

You stay very quiet and the people run on, unaware of your presence. You drop to the ground and then head in the opposite direction. You wander out of the forest and on through meadows filled with yellow flowers.

After traveling a long way, you are about to lie down and rest, when up ahead you notice a strange, silver dome as big as a house. You walk up to it and a door slides open. It is filled with a dim green light, but you cannot see what else may be inside.

If you go in, turn to page 75.

If you stay away, turn to page 76.

You sink deeper and deeper. You wiggle and squirm, but it is too late. Glug, glug, glug.

The End

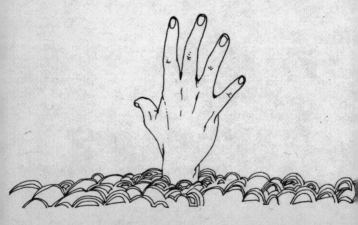

You roll over and over across the slurpy, ooshy, wet sand. In a moment you feel firm ground. You stand up dirty and wet, but happy to be alive.

"Very smart," says a voice a few feet away. You turn around, and standing nearby is a boy who looks about your age. He is brown from the sun, and his hair is like a mop. He tells you he was shipwrecked a year ago and that he catches animals that walk into the quicksand. He has built a raft and invites you to put to sea with him in hopes that the current will carry you down the coast to civilization.

If you go on the raft, turn to page 77.

If you stay, turn to page 78.

The fish tastes good after all.

The pirate smiles and says, "You didn't have to eat the fish, I just wanted to see if you have a brain in your head. Since you do, I'm glad you've come along. I've got a boat rigged and ready to leave for the Galapagos Islands. I can make it if I have another hand aboard, and you seem fit to take your turn at the helm. Avast! Let's load 'er up and be out of here."

He takes you to a cove where a crude sailboat lies at anchor.

If you go to sea with the pirate, turn to page 79.

If you run away at the first chance, turn to page 80.

The pirate is furious at you. You run up a steep hill, and he lumbers after you. You dart across a rock ledge. He comes right on your heels. You hear a crumbling sound and then a scream. He has fallen twenty feet onto the rocks below. You climb down and look at him cautiously. He is almost dead.

"I tried to kill you," he murmurs, "and killed myself. Now I'll try to help you—and maybe help myself. Under that waterfall, there is a cave. Crawl in and follow the long tunnel. Near the end is a sandy spot. Dig, and you will find the largest diamond in the world. Then go on and in a few feet you will come out to safety and . . ." Suddenly the pirate dies.

If you follow his advice, turn to page 81.

If you do not follow his advice, turn to page 82.

The pirate is friendly and jolly. He is evidently delighted to see you. You help him cook the fish. It is the best you ever ate.

"Now, my friend," says he, "I suppose you would like to go home. I wish I could join you, but since I am wanted for robbing five towns, I can't. But I will guide you to a village where you can board a boat for home."

The next day, you and the pirate begin a long journey through swamps and over mountains. It is a week before you can look down from the hill on the village. You shake hands and thank him.

He looks at you sternly and then smiles and says simply, "Good luck."

The End

You hide in the woods and fall asleep. When you awaken, looking down on you is a skinny old man with a bushy white beard.

"Do not fear, my child. Here time goes in circles. If you stand up, you will soon lie down again."

"Does that mean," you ask, "if I come to this island, I will soon go home again?"

The man nods his head up and down.

If you listen further, turn to page 84.

If you run away, turn to page 85.

When you walk up close to the old man, he grabs you by the shoulder.

"Listen to me," he says. "If I had as much food as I have gold, I would be a happy man. If only you could help me . . ."

"Maybe I can get help, if you tell me what you want," you say.

"Maybe you can," says the old man. "Walk along the shore to the broken boulders. Then take the trail through the pine forest to the village. But don't forget me!"

You follow the directions and get to the village. It is located on a harbor. There are many fishing boats tied up along the waterfront. In the harbor a large sailing ship is riding at anchor. You see some sailors from the ship bargaining with the natives.

If you tell them about the old man, turn to page 86.

If you do not tell them about him, turn to page 87.

You run down the hill. You find the beach and follow the shore line for mile after mile. You live on crabs, clams, and seaweed. It rains a great deal, and you get enough water to drink from ponds not far in from the beach. After a few days, you come upon a camp. There are about twelve people. They have lots of equipment—telescopes, radios, guns. They are Australians.

"What are you doing here?" they ask.

"What are you doing here?" you ask.

"We have been looking for the famous explorer, Henry Gelundersprung, and we are about to give up. We will take you home."

If you tell them about the old man, turn to page 88.

If not, turn to page 89.

You run higher and finally have to climb up on the high snow-covered ridge. The warrior starts after you, but stops when he gets to the snow. You see he is afraid and that you are safe.

He calls out, "Don't hurt me." He thinks you must have magic power to be able to survive in the snow. You laugh at him and then continue on over the high slopes and down into a green valley. Ahead of you is a peaceful village. Some friendly people run out to greet you. For the first time you feel safe on Sugarcane Island.

The End

The warrior rushes after you and with one great lunge hurls you over the cliff. You fall onto a ledge and lie there, feeling battered and bruised. The fierce warrior thinks you are dead and starts back to his village.

After a while you pick yourself up. Fortunately, you did not break any bones.

If you try to go on, turn to page 90.

If you head back to the native village, turn to page 91.

You feel it is better to take your chances on the rushing river than with the unpredictable islanders. You shove your raft out into the river. The islanders cheer. They laugh as they see you are drifting down toward the waterfall. You pole along trying to get to the other side. Suddenly, you are swirling through the rapids. You tumble over the waterfall. But you grab a log and go careening on downstream. You are not hurt, and the islanders are left far behind. After a while the current slows and you can catch your breath.

If you paddle to the shore, turn to page 92.

If you continue on down the river, turn to page 93.

The islanders are furious. Two of them carry you over their shoulders through the jungle. They take you to a cliff and throw you over the edge. You fall down, down, down. Your eyes are closed. You dare not look. Then, splash into the water. The wind is knocked out of you; you come up to the surface gasping for air. You are in a beautiful lagoon. The water is warm and clear. You look up and see the islanders cheering at the top of the cliff. You have passed the test. They think you have magic powers because you did not drown.

The islanders take you back to the village, and you all have a great feast of sugarcane cake and pink grapes. Later, they show you the way to a village by the sea, where you can wait for a boat to take you back to San Francisco.

The End

You wonder how to escape. If you just run away, the islanders might track you and find you in the forest. There seems to be only one chance. The village is in a valley next to a volcano which has been belching forth clouds of yellow-brown smoke. The islanders are afraid of it. You decide that if you run up the side of the volcano they will not dare to follow you.

Early the next morning even more smoke is pouring out. The islanders mumble nervously. You run through the woods toward the volcano and climb up its slopes. The islanders follow. Just as they are about to catch you there is a rumble. Smoke and fire spit out of the mountain. The islanders scream and run back toward their village.

If you try to climb further and get to the other side of the volcano, turn to page 96.

If you run back with the islanders, turn to page 97.

You stay on in Abagun. You grow strong and learn to hunt and fish. You learn the secrets of the forest and the stories of the stars. It is a happy life, but you miss your home.

Years later, visiting scientists wandering through the forest come upon the village and are captured. The chief tells them they can never leave, but they do not seem to mind. To your surprise they tell the chief they will be perfectly happy to stay forever. One of the scientists, however, takes you aside. "Stay close to me tomorrow," he says.

The next day at noontime, a great helicopter swirls down from the sky. The islanders are frightened and scatter in all directions. You follow the scientists up to the helicopter and climb aboard. In a moment you are safely on your way home.

The End

You sit with the sailor trying to think up something magic. It seems hopeless. But after a while the sailor tells you he has thought of something. The next morning the two fierce-looking islanders bring you and the sailor before the chief. "I can talk without speaking," says the sailor to the chief.

"That would be real magic," says the chief.

Then the sailor takes a piece of paper and writes on it the words "Raise your right hand." Without opening his mouth he holds up the paper so that you can read it. Naturally, you raise your right hand. The chief is amazed at this magic way of talking. He tells you that you can join the tribe, or, if you prefer, they will take you to the next village.

If you join the tribe, turn to page 99.

If you decide to go on to the next village, turn to page 100.

You run quickly between two huts and dash into the brush. Suddenly, you feel the searing pain of a spear in your back. You sink to the ground —finished for good.

The End

You dash into the middle of the village. The islanders are huddled in the rain. They are praying. They seem to be afraid of the storm. You are afraid yourself, but you walk among the people calling out "Hello there!"

The islanders stand up in awe. There is one final thunder clap and bolt of lightning and then the rain stops. The storm is over.

The islanders think you are a "Storm God." They give you a banquet of sugarcane cake and pink grapes and a soft bed to sleep on. The next day, though, some of the natives become suspicious. They come around and make faces at you.

Turn to page 98.

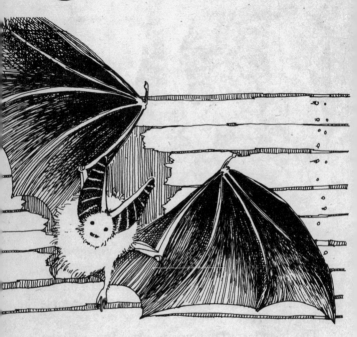

You hide. The storm passes. You are wet, cold, and hungry. The village is quiet. You must move on. You trample through the forest, then climb a hill. In the distance you can see the ocean. If only you could be back on shipboard with Dr. Frisbee . . .

Then you notice a strange shape on the beach. You walk toward it. It is the wreck of a ship which the sea cast up on the beach like a toy.

You walk around it. The hatches are shut tight, but there is a hole in the side. You peer in. It is dark. A bat comes flying out past your ear.

If you decide to crawl in through the hole, turn to page 103

If you decide not to crawl in through the hole, turn to page 105.

Everyone goes to bed. You sit wondering what you can do to help in the battle with the other tribe. Two ideas occur to you. One idea is to advise the tribe to leave the village and wait in ambush for the enemy. Another possibility is to attack the village of the other tribe to catch them off guard.

If you decide to advise an ambush, turn to page 106.

If you decide to advise preventive attack, turn to page 107.

You say you can't help, and that you better just keep out of the way.

Turn to page 107.

You stuff your pockets with jewels and run down the path. As you round the corner, you see in front of you three bearded men with packs on their backs. One has a shovel, one has a pick, and one has a map. Each of them have guns. You hide behind a bush.

One man says, "Drat. The map is wrong. The treasure is not here! I'm going to strangle the man who sold us this map."

If you talk to the men and tell them of the treasure, turn to page 108.

If you talk to the men but do not tell them of the treasure, turn to page 109.

If you stay hidden, turn to page 110.

You wait and wait. Finally you fall asleep. You begin to dream. In the dream there are five lions stalking you from different directions. You wake up in a fright. Five islanders with spears are standing over you. They search you and drag you back to camp. You are led up the chief's hut.

"Clubub! Clubub! Clubub!" scream some of the wild people. But the chief comes and holds up his hand. He speaks the native tongue and calms the crowd, then he talks to you in English.

"You are the first stranger who found the jewels and did not take any. We will guide you to a village where you can board a boat to take you to America, or if you are willing to find your own way, you may have a large diamond to keep."

If you choose the first offer, turn to page 112.

If you choose the second offer, turn to page 113.

The secret potion tastes awful, and you at once wish you had not tasted it. You feel queasy and sit down. Soon the witches seem to grow larger and whirl around until all you can see are swirling shapes of color, and you feel yourself rising up in the air and falling, swaying from side to side. You hear a rhythmic swish, swish, slap of running water.

A voice calls out "Hey, it's time for dinner."

It is Dr. Frisbee! You were dreaming all the time, and you realize you are still on your ship headed for the Galapagos Islands.

The End

When you refuse to drink the secret potion, the witches are angry. They dance around you screaming and chanting and waving their arms—as if to put a curse on you. You feel angry and kick over their cauldrons. Suddenly the witches are gone, and there in front of you is a great turtle.

"You have freed me from the curse of Andaga," says the turtle, "What can I do for you?"

"Take me to a boat which will go to America," you say.

The turtle is silent but waddles over to you.

Turn to page 94.

You just manage to scramble up the steep part of the turtle's shell and get on top. The turtle, who acts as if he knows where he is going, lumbers along through the meadow and down a little hill and splash—is in the water and swimming. You feel as if you are riding a tiny round raft. You look around. You are on a broad stream, and here and there you see long, green crocodiles. Your turtle keeps clear of them. Suddenly, the stream reaches the sea. The turtle is about to swim on out into the ocean!

If you stay on, turn to page 114.

If you dive off, turn to page 115.

You follow the turtle all the way to the ocean. It stands there at the water's edge and looks around at you and blinks in the sunshine. If only Dr. Frisbee could see the turtle. Its head sticks up almost as high as yours.

Suddenly, the turtle walks into the water and swims away. You are once again alone and hungry, thirsty, and tired. You are too tired even to climb up the hill. You rest a while, wondering if you will survive for long in such a place.

Turn to page 5.

The coconut drums beat ba da, ba da. Your new friends smile at you. You have good feelings about them. After a while, you sleep. When you wake up, only one of the group is still there.

"This is a beautiful place," you say.

"Yes," he replies. "I am happy you have been here, but you must go."

"Why?" you ask.

"Because nothing changes here. It is paradise, and therefore it is death. Take this fruit, follow the path by the sea, and you will reach a friendly village in three days.

If you go on, turn to page 116.

If you stay, turn to page 117.

The islanders are delighted. They give you some sugarcane cake and pink grapes. You sleep well. The next day they take you to a house in a much larger village located on a pretty harbor.

There you visit with a friendly family until, a few weeks later, a ship bound for San Francisco stops by at the harbor. The captain offers you a ride. You bid your new friends goodbye and soon you are on your way home to America.

The End

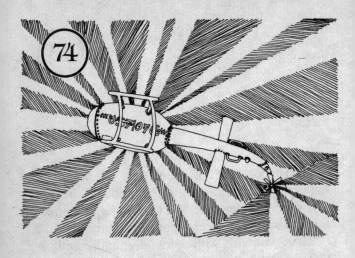

When you refuse to stand on your head, the people are very angry. They grab you and tie your feet and hang you upside down. You have never been so scared in your life. Finally, they let you down, but you are kept a prisoner, and each day forced to hang upside down for an hour.

One day, while you are hanging, there is a strange, loud, whirring, put-put-put-put sound. The islanders look up and run off screaming. Then all is quiet. You call for help. In a moment some men in khaki uniforms have found you and cut your ropes. It is a helicopter rescue team looking for survivors of the tidal wave.

In a few minutes your helicopter is in the air and you are on your way to the Galapagos Islands where Dr. Frisbee is waiting for you.

The End

Inside the green-lit dome, everything seems hard and shiny and clean, but almost immediately the light fades and it is dark. You close your eyes, and it seems to be light.

Then the bright dome seems to grow as big and blue as the sky. The light is brilliant. You look around—startled. It is the sun! You have been dreaming on your deck chair—still on your way to the Galapagos Islands.

The End

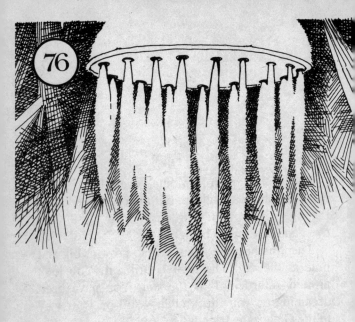

You run from the great dome. With a roar of rocket fire, it lifts off from the earth and softly floats away up into the blue sky. You stand there watching. Suddenly, some islanders appear out of the jungle. They walk up to you, holding out their hands. They give you coconut milk and sugarcane candy and molasses cake and fruit punch and bracelets of emeralds and sapphires. They think you are a Space God. You live in their village for a few days. Then you learn of another village—a few days walk—where ships visit from other lands. You bid your new friends farewell and start on the trip back home.

The End

Your friend has made water bags from animal skins, and the two of you lash these to your raft with vines. You eat a big meal and drink as much water as you can from a nearby spring. Then, with two flat sticks for paddles, you push the raft out to sea.

The current takes you rapidly along the coast. You look to a rocky point of land, but then the wind blows you off and in a few minutes you are out on the open sea.

For a day and a night you drift on, wondering how long your food and water will last. The next morning, the early light reveals a great island ahead rising from the sea. You see fishing boats, and one is headed toward you. You know you will soon be rescued.

The End

You help your new friend gather coconuts and lash them to the raft together with water bags he had made from animal skins. He teaches you how to build a fire from flint stones and how to catch animals. Finally, you help push the raft out into the water and wave goodbye. It drifts quickly away along the coast of the island. You wonder where it will take him.

During the following months, you live well and grow stronger, discovering new things every day about the plants and strange creatures that live at the edge of the sea.

After many months have passed, you, too, begin to build a raft.

The End

You put out to sea in a fair breeze. The boat moves nicely through the water, but you wonder how it will take the heavy seas, running on the open ocean.

"You know, we're only fifty miles from an island with lots of rum," says the pirate. "Come on and lash yourself to the ship with this line or a wave will carry you off to the sharks."

Soon the boat is riding up and down in the foamy mists of the sea. You wonder if you and the pirate will ever make it to friendly shores.

You make it.

The End

The night before the day you and the pirate have decided to set sail, you wait until he is asleep. Then you slip away and run along the dark beach to get as far as possible before he discovers you are gone. Finally, you lie down to rest. You are awakened by the bright light of the sun. You feel thirsty, scared, and lonely.

Turn to page 5.

You crawl into the cave and wander along the tunnel. Your knees and elbows are scraped by sharp rocks. It is cold and damp, and you wish you had not listened to the pirate. The tunnel is so tight you cannot turn around. It is dark and you are scared.

You lie flat to rest, stretching your arms forward. The ground is sandy under your hands. You dig with your fingers, and almost immediately you feel it—a diamond as big as an egg!

You crawl on through the tunnel. You see light ahead. In a few moments you are out again in the sunshine. You are on a hill overlooking a blue-green lagoon. Anchored close to the shore is a two-masted schooner, flying a United States flag. You know now that you will find your way home. And you still have the enormous diamond.

The End

Not trusting the pirate, you sit down to think. You are so hungry that you eat some of his fish anyway. You wander on and come to a meadow filled with sugarcane.

For months you live on sugarcane and coconut and fish. One day when peering through the woods into an open glade, you see a strange man on his hands and knees. He is holding a magnifying glass.

"Hello," you call out.

"Hello!" he says. "I'm Dr. Waddle. I have just about given up looking for the lost ape of Pacifica."

You have a long talk with Dr. Waddle and find he is a scientist like Dr. Frisbee. In fact it turns out Dr. Frisbee and Dr. Waddle are old friends, and soon you and Dr. Waddle are on your way to his ship, anchored in a nearby harbor. The next day you sail for home. As the ship heads out to sea, you stand on the stern and wave goodbye to Sugarcane Island.

The End

"When will that be?" you ask.

"It depends," says the man, "which circle your time runs in."

"How do you know all this?" you say.

"My time has turned into a knot, and I do nothing but the same thing. I always have and always will, but you will circle back."

You back away from the strange man and run into the woods, where you come upon a stream and once again find a pirate fishing. It is the same pirate, or another? You cannot tell. You sit and watch him.

Turn to page 23.

85

You dash off into the woods and wander on and on looking for food, people—anything. Suddenly you are startled by a long green snake dangling down from a tree right in front of your nose. You run on at full speed.

Turn to page 25.

You lead the sailors back to the old man. He thanks you and says that he has discovered buried treasure but that he cannot get back to a village without help.

He leads you to the treasure. The sailors eagerly dig into the ground until they find it.

The old man keeps half and gives you a one-quarter share and divides the rest among the sailors. You return with the sailors to their boat. In a few days you are all headed back home.

The End

The sailors take you back to the S.S. *Mary Ann,* a big, green banana boat bound for San Francisco. In a few days you are heading home. The seas are smooth, and you enjoy exploring the boat, but you wonder whether you should have told someone about the old man—and what would have happened if you had.

The End

The Australians tell you the old man you met is Henry Gelundersprung. You agree to lead them back to him.

As you walk along the track, you hear gunfire. Someone is shouting from behind some large boulders. The Australians fire back. A bullet whistles through your hair. In a while all is still. The Australians say there are dangerous bandits on the island. You continue cautiously up the trail to where you found Henry Gelundersprung. "Hello-o-o" calls a voice. It is Henry.

The Australians guide you and Henry back to a friendly village. Henry sees that you get a share of his gold to take back to America.

The End

The Australians take you to their ship. They seem sad about not finding the missing explorer. The ship sails to the Galapagos Islands, where happily you find your old friend Dr. Frisbee. The boat survived the tidal wave. He had thought you had drowned and is happy to see you. He captured some strange looking turtles. Soon the two of you are on your way back to San Francisco. You are happy to be on your way home, but you will always wonder who the old man was and what became of him.

The End

90

You struggle up over the mountain pass to the top. You are cold and tired. You see a beautiful green valley below, but you are too cold and tired to go on.

The End

You make it back to the village. The chief is amazed to hear your story. The evil warrior is punished, and the chief and three of the best warriors guide you over the mountain pass down to the village and to safety.

"Now," said the chief, "our people will never be afraid of snow again."

The End

You paddle to the other shore. It is full of sharp thickets. You struggle to get through them. You are scratched, but you make it through and out onto a broad meadow. You find a trail and follow it, hoping to find your way to a friendly village. Suddenly a band of islanders rushes out and seizes you.

Turn to page 29.

You drift along a day and a night. There are no more rapids. You pass tall trees with huge, floppy leaves. Green and purple birds fly about over your head.

At last the current brings you a friendly village. The villagers tell you of a boat leaving in a few days for the Galapagos Islands. The captain welcomes you as a passenger. After a week's trip at sea, you arrive. The captain has radioed ahead, and good old Dr. Frisbee is waiting on the dock to meet you.

The End

You climb on the turtle. Without seeming to notice you, it moves swiftly along. It is indeed a magic turtle, although it will not talk to you any more. After an hour's journey the turtle reaches a beach and heads down into the sea. You hold on tight to its knobby back.

If you ride on with the turtle into the sea, turn to page 114.

If you hop off, turn to page 95.

You roll off the turtle's back and watch it swim on out to sea. You walk up the beach and into the brush. You realize you are thirsty and hungry.

Turn to page 12.

You run along the edge of the volcano trying to get across to the other side. The smoke is so thick you can hardly breathe. The ground rumbles, and you can feel underground explosions through your feet. Finally, you find a path skirting around the mountain. You run down the mountain as fast as you can. At last you can breathe fresh air. Then there is a great explosion behind you, and you hear the sound of crumbling rocks and falling trees. The volcano has blown off the other side of the mountain. You do not know it, but the village of Abagun now lies buried under molten lava.

You find your way along a path reaching to the ocean and wander along the shore for two days. Finally, you reach a friendly village by a lagoon shielded from the surf by a coral reef. You live there with a kind family. They tell you that every month a ship visits from Mexico and that if you wish to go home the captain will be glad to take you. You are happy to hear that!

The End

You run back to the islanders. The volcano belches forth. The black lava pours down the mountain toward their village. The air smells of hot sulphur. The islanders no longer try to hurt you. They pray and chant in hopes that their village will not be destroyed.

In a little while a fresh cool wind blows across the fields. The air clears. Everyone looks up. The lava flow has stopped. The mountain is quiet. The villagers come and bow to you. They think you saved them from destruction. They give you rare jewels in thanks for the help they think you have given them. The next day they show you a hidden trail to a village where you can wait for a visiting boat bound for America.

The End

98

You realize that it would be wise to leave and ask one of the islanders where a village might be that ships come to visit.

"To the west," says he; "three days walk is a village with strange pale men with noisy machines. To the east is a wide river. What lies beyond it none of us know."

If you go west, turn to page 101.

If you go east, turn to page 102.

You join the tribe and learn to fish and hunt and play its games. After a few months you feel as quick as a fox and as strong as a bear. You miss your home and family though, and one day you set out through the jungle to find your way to civilization.

After traveling two days and two nights, you come to a sparkling river. The water is cool and clear. Across the river are hundreds of coconut trees. You are hungry.

Turn to page 38.

The islanders take you through miles and miles of forest and over mountains. You camp out each night and march by day. It is tiring, but there is plenty of sugarcane to munch on along the way and the islanders know where to find cool, clear water.

Finally, one day, you look down on a large village built on the edge of a sparkling bay rimmed by coral reefs. There are ponies pulling carts about and even a few jeeps. Anchored in the harbor is a three masted schooner flying the American flag. You feel sure that the captain will invite you to come with them and only wonder whether the boat will be returning to America or traveling on to other islands. Either way sounds good to you, for you are ready to leave Sugarcane Island.

The End

You leave quietly without saying goodbye, taking a supply of food. You wander west through forest, meadow, swamps, and over rocky ridges. You see many strange animals and more than once dash away from one of the large green snakes that inhabit the island. You live on coconuts and wild sugarcane. Many days pass before you climb a ridge from which you can look down at a village where you see people riding donkeys, bikes, and jeeps. You feel happy, because you know that the ships that deliver these things can take you back home.

The End

You walk to the east, trying always to head toward the sun in the morning and to have the sun on your back in the afternoon. But often it is cloudy, and you begin to wonder whether you have really traveled east or not. One morning you smell a salty breeze. You hurry on to a sandy hill and look out at sea. You walk onto the beach and then lie down. You feel very tired and hungry. But you get up. You know you must go on.

Turn to page 5.

You grope along inside the ship. Several times you slip and fall in the total darkness. You brush against some soft, slimy things. You wonder if you can find your way out again. You find a door, but it will not open. Next to the door you feel cold metal, then glass. You grab hold. It is a battery powered lantern. The battery is still good.

In a moment you have light. You search around inside the boat and find food, water, canned juice, and, finally, the ship's radio. You learn to use it, and send out a distress call. A voice on a distant ship answers. "We can tell where you are from your radio signals," the voice says. "We'll send help."

"Thanks," you say.

The End

You stay at the edge of the beach, nervously wondering if another tidal wave may come. You live on coconuts, but you are too tired to explore the island further. You use all your energy just trying to find enough food to stay alive. You wonder if you ever will be rescued. Finally, you are too tired to care. Years later, explorers find your bones in the sand.

The End

The chief is enthusiastic about your idea of an ambush. It has never been tried before. At sunrise your group spreads out behind rocks and brush along the trail between the two villages. The enemy advances. Your tribe attacks from ambush, spears the enemy tribesmen before they realize what has happened, wins the battle, and brings peace to their village.

You are a hero. The villagers give you jewels and gold and help you find your way to another friendly village where you can wait for a ship to take you home.

The End

The chief does not like what you say. He becomes angry. The villagers tie you to a stake and say they will burn you alive when they come back from the battle. They leave. You are alone. You wait all day. You cannot wiggle free. Every hope seems lost.

Then, as the sun is going down, there are great whoops and cries and a strange new crowd of people rushes into the village. It is the enemy tribe. They have won the battle. They rush up and untie you. The chief says "Any prisoner of theirs is a friend of ours."

In a few days they help you find your way to a friendly village where you can wait for a ship to take you home.

The End

The men shake you excitedly. "Where is the treasure?" they cry.

You feel you have no choice but to take them there.

They shove you aside and seize the chest, greedily sifting the jewels through their fingers. You hide in the bushes. Suddenly a band of islanders appears. They seize the men and carry them off screaming and yelling.

You are left alone. But you see the map lying on the ground. With it you find your way to a little fishing village, where you are given food and shelter. The next day you are taken by boat to an island where ships visit from the United States. When finally you return home, your pockets are still full of precious jewels.

The End

The men are surprised to see you and even more surprised to hear of your strange adventure. They ask you if you know of any hidden treasure. You tell them you do not.

The leader says, "It is useless. We have been cheated. There is no buried treasure. Well, follow us and you shall find your way home."

You follow the men for over a mile, barely able to keep up with them. Finally, the four of you reach a harbor and row out to a large motor boat. After a two day trip, you reach another island. The boat ties up to a dock. The men tell you how to find your way to an airport. Just as you say goodbye, a diamond slips out of your pocket. Quickly, they search you and take all your jewels, cursing you. You run away from them.

Eventually, you reach home, happy to be back with your family, but sad you were not able to bring with you any of the treasure of Sugarcane Island.

The End

You stay hidden.

After a while, the men go away. You sit there wondering if you dare take more jewels. Suddenly, some islanders with spears rush out of the bush.

They take you back to the camp. The chief comes out and speaks to you.

"You are honest. We watched and saw that you took no treasure."

"But I did," you say.

"Then you are truly honest, for you admitted it. You may keep the treasure," he says with a smile.

"It means nothing to us. For our jewels are the stars in the sky and the glistening waves of the sea."

The next day the islanders guide you to a village where you can wait for a ship that will take you back to America.

The End

The islanders take you with them down a path to the harbor. You sail with them to another island not far away where you can board an American ship. Then they bid you goodbye and return to their village and their treasure.

The End

You put the enormous diamond the chief has given you in your pocket and head into the jungle. It looks hopeless. After a while, you come back and find the chief and tell him you cannot find your way out.

"We shall show you," says the chief, "but you must prove yourself." They blindfold you and lead you on a march up and down many hills. Finally, you feel sand under your feet. You are close to the ocean. They wait until you are asleep. When you wake up, you are lying high on a great sand dune. Behind you is a broad sloping beach, ahead of you a meadow of tall reeds. Beyond it is a high rocky hill. You are hungry and thirsty. There are no signs of life. You look out at the ocean and see nothing but endless blue water. You are all alone. You realize you are at the place where the tidal wave first cast you up on Sugarcane Island.

If you decide to walk along the beach, turn to page 5.

If you decide to climb the rocky hill, turn to page 6.

You ride along further and further from shore. The turtle suddenly dives, leaving you alone in the thrashing waves. You do not see the turtle again, but you do see a huge shark swimming toward you. In only a moment the shark has finished his dinner—of you.

The End

You dive off and swim as fast as you can to the nearest shore. You climb up and find a trail through the forest. You wonder whether it was made by people or by animals.

After a while, you come to a clear blue pond. You see some fish that you think you might catch for supper. You hear a sound behind you. You look around and see a large animal charging at you. It looks like a tiger without any stripes. It is too late to escape.

The End

You follow the path. Each day you eat one of the strange fruits and save the pits. They give you so much energy and strength you feel as if you could battle a tiger.

At sunset on the day you have eaten the last of the wonderful fruit, you reach a village where you meet friendly people. By the village is a harbor. One day a visiting ship from the States drops anchor and sends a boat ashore for supplies. The captain offers you a ride. A month later you happily walk through the door of your own home. Later you plant the pits of the strange fruit, but they are a kind that grows only on Sugarcane Island.

The End

You do not believe your new friend. Why should anyone ever leave such a pleasant place? Day after day passes in the grove of the strange fruit. There are many others there. Everyone looks happy, but no one talks or plays. Soon you forget how long you have been there. You feel as if you are floating on a cloud. You become weaker, until you no longer have the strength to leave the valley of the pleasure fruit. Dimly you realize that you should have left before it was too late.

The End

ABOUT THE AUTHOR

Edward Packard was born in Huntington, New York, and graduated from Princeton and Columbia Law School. He lives with his wife in New York City and practices law in New York and Connecticut. He conceived of **SUGARCANE ISLAND** while thinking up bedtime stories for his children Caroline, Andrea, and Wells.

ABOUT THE ILLUSTRATOR

Barbara Carter lives in Randolph, Vermont, and has been working as an illustrator for several years. In addition to writing and illustrating her own children's books, she raises goats and cows.

Meet McGurk!

Got a mystery to solve? Just ask McGurk. He heads the McGurk Detective Organization, and he and his supersleuths—Wanda, Willie, Joey, and Brains Bellingham—can unravel just about anything! They've solved the puzzle of the ruthless bird killer, tracked down a missing newsboy, traced an <u>invisible</u> dog, and cracked the case of a mysterious robbery.

Can you solve these tricky cases?
Follow the clues and
match wits with master-mind McGurk!

The McGURK MYSTERIES, by E. W. Hildick,
illustrated by Iris Schweitzer:

———	42005	$1.75	DEADLINE FOR McGURK	#1
———	41404	$1.75	THE CASE OF THE CONDEMNED CAT	#2
———	41405	$1.75	THE CASE OF THE NERVOUS NEWSBOY	#3
———	41454	$1.75	THE GREAT RABBIT RIP OFF	#4
———	41406	$1.75	THE CASE OF THE INVISIBLE DOG	#5
———	56014	$1.50	THE CASE OF THE SECRET SCRIBBLER	#6
———	56064	$1.75	THE CASE OF THE PHANTOM FROG	#7

There's No Stopping
Danny Dunn!

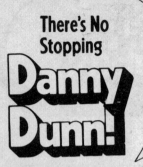

Danny Dunn, science fiction hero, with his friends,
Irene and Joe, can't stay away from mystery and
adventure. They have shrunk to the size of insects,
traveled back in time, sunk to the ocean floor,
and rocketed through outer space!

The DANNY DUNN books,
by Jay Williams and Raymond Abrashkin:

ARCHWAY PAPERBACKS from Pocket Books